# LAUGH-ALONG

# NURSERY RHYMES

Rookie
Nursery
Rhymes™

Children's Press®
An Imprint of Scholastic Inc.

Library of Congress Cataloging-in-Publication Data

Names: Reid, Mick. 1958- | Farías, Carolina, illustrator. | Hefferan, Rob, illustrator.
Title: Laugh-along nursery rhymes.
Description: New York, NY : Children's Press, an imprint of Scholastic Inc.,
[2016] | ?2017 | Series: Rookie nursery rhymes | Summary: Includes three
traditional nursery rhymes, illustrated by different artists.
Identifiers: LCCN 2016006310| ISBN 9780531228791 (library binding) | ISBN 9780531229651 (pbk.)
Subjects: LCSH: Nursery rhymes. | Children's poetry. | CYAC: Nursery rhymes.
Classification: LCC PZ8.3 .L347 2016 | DDC 398.8—dc23 LC record available at http://lccn.loc.gov/2016006310

Produced by Spooky Cheetah Press
Design by Book & Look

Printed in China 62

SCHOLASTIC, CHILDREN'S PRESS, ROOKIE NURSERY RHYMES™ and associated logos
are trademarks and/or registered trademarks of Scholastic Inc.

2 3 4 5 6 7 8 9 10 R 25 24 23 22 21 20 19 18 17

Illustrations by Mick Reid (Hickory, Dickory, Dock), Carolina Farías (Humpty Dumpty),
Rob Hefferan (This Little Piggy), and pp 6–12, 14–20, 22–28 (wooden bar) Venimo/Shutterstock

Scholastic Inc., 557 Broadway, New York, NY 10012.

# TABLE OF CONTENTS

# HICKORY, DICKORY, DOCK

Illustrated by Mick Reid

Hickory, dickory, dock,

the mouse ran up the clock.

The clock struck one.

The mouse ran down.

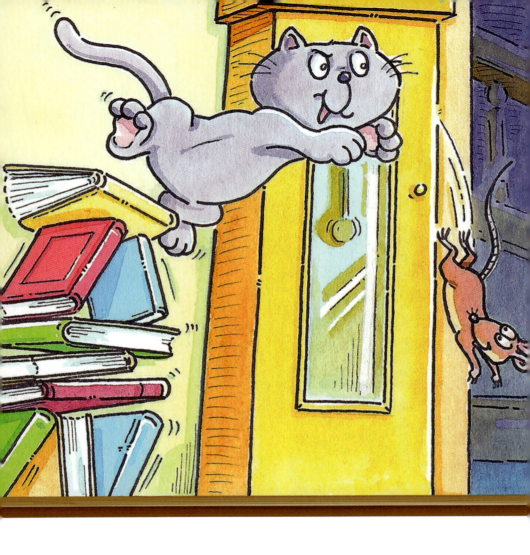

Hickory,

dickory,

dock.

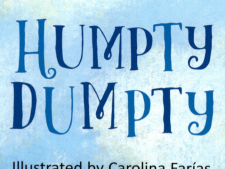

# HUMPTY DUMPTY

## Illustrated by Carolina Farías

**Listen to the audio here:**

http://www.scholastic.com/NR8

# Humpty Dumpty

sat on a wall.

# Humpty Dumpty

had a great fall.

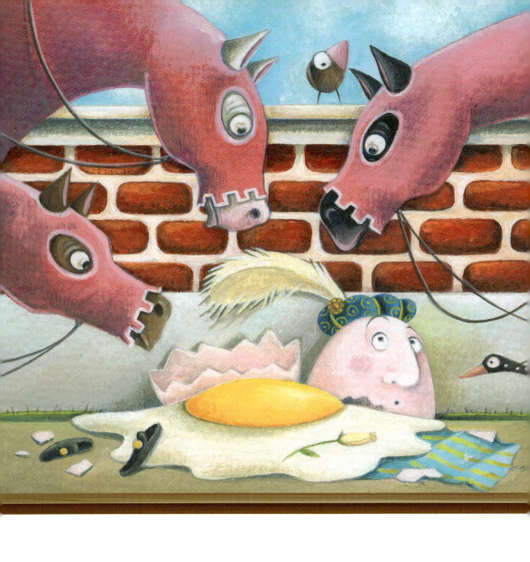

All the King's horses

and all the King's men

couldn't put Humpty
together again.

# THIS LITTLE PIGGY

Illustrated by Rob Hefferan

TO MARKET

This little piggy went to market.

This little piggy stayed home.

This little piggy had roast beef.

This little piggy had none.

And this little piggy

cried wee-wee-wee...

all the way home.

# FUN WITH

# NURSERY
# RHYMES

**FUN WITH**

## Hickory, Dickory, Dock
### Pages 5 to 12

A cat reading a book? That's just one of the many silly things that happen in this story!

## Take another look through the book.

- What color is the book the cat is reading?

- How many books of this color can you count throughout the story?

- Where do all the books end up at the end of the story?

## Humpty Dumpty
### Pages 13 to 20

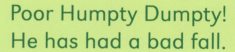

Poor Humpty Dumpty!
He has had a bad fall.

## Go back to the story and count:

- How many birds do you see flying around Humpty Dumpty?

- How many towers are on the castle behind him?

31

## This Little Piggy
### Pages 21 to 28

There are so many things in this book to make us laugh!

## Look back at the pictures to find some silly-looking pigs.

- Can you find a piggy wearing glasses?
- Can you find a piggy wearing long earrings?
- Do pigs usually wear clothes?